ESCAPE TO INDRIEG

A journey through the
imagination and beyond …

Daryl Ainsworth

INTRODUCING INDRIEG

How the island got its name!

For as long as I can remember, and a little bit before that, I've been known by my family and friends to frequently disappear into my own 'world', or as they say 'island'. This island is an island of dreams and boundless possibilities, blended seamlessly with impossibilities. Of course, it has coral sand beaches, waterfalls, lakes and palm trees - what half-decent island wouldn't have right? ... but this island also has a shed and that's where you'll find me! I'm not lazing about taking in the sunshine and the stunning scenery, much as I'd like, no, I'm sat in my shed with the shutters down and the fan on, working hard! This stuff doesn't just do itself; no, someone has to do it and that someone is me!

Indrieg didn't used to have a name, or maybe it was just that I was unaware of its name. Either way its name didn't matter - I was far too busy working in my shed to care if my island had a name, or indeed what that name was.

Then, one day, I was playing a game of Scrabble with my closest friends, whilst paying frequent visits to my island between moves. The letters before me were: 'I-N-D-R-I-E-G'. Not being able to make a move I showed them to my friend for help, who then informed me that 'INDRIEG' was coincidentally also the name of my island too. So 'INDRIEG' the island officially became!

Welcome to 'Indrieg', my island!

MY SAFE PLACE

The Island

Indreig, as an island, is rich in flora, fauna, vegetation, and geological features. It's rich in practically anything, and usually, at the precise moment that it needs to be rich in it. It's a bit like a paradise, but with a twist, and when I can work out what that twist is, I'm reasonably determined have a go at untwisting it! In the meanwhile, I'll just accept the twist as one of the many quirky features that makes my island so unique and intriguing.

My hideaway

As I've already said, when I'm on Indrieg I'm in my shed, working hard. So, I thought I'd better tell you a little about the shed, being as that's where you'll find me.

It's not a big or a fancy shed, it's not even a particularly well fitted-out shed, it just has the basics - just what I need to get the job done, nothing more than that really. It's not one of those sheds that's bigger on the inside either - if anything it's a little smaller on the inside, but only by about six inches.

Palms, waterfalls, dunes …

It has a small window, which from my stool, frames one of the most stunning views on Indrieg. You can see the stream wending its way through the palm groves, down to the lake, with the dunes and sea in the middle distance and birds diving into waterfalls, re-emerging with whatever birds dive into waterfalls for, in their beaks. When the sun is in just the right place, which it does tend to be, rainbows glisten in the mist over the falls. I've often thought it is possibly the most stunning view you could wish to behold, if, that is, the shutters weren't down and held firmly in place by a twisted rusty nail.

My undignified arrivals!

The shed doesn't have a door, that's simply because it doesn't really need one. When I arrive I just land, in an undignified heap, on my stool! The springs squeak and groan a bit these days, when I do - not sure if it's the springs at fault or if I'm a little heavier than I used to be. I switch the fan back on and I'm straight to work. I don't mess about, as I have a lot to be getting on with, and I can't say how long I have, to be doing it, so it's down to business.

Abandoned projects appreciated

Very important issues get contemplated here in great depth, just occasionally important issues are even resolved too - when I say 'resolved' I mean 'largely' resolved, or resolved 'in principle'. I suppose, what I'm getting at, is, that *nothing* ever gets finished here. But that's completely okay. Indrieg is a place of inspiration, bright ideas and bold, if flawed, beginnings and best intentions. Stuff doesn't have to be finished, no pressure here, it can just lie about until it's picked up again and may even be taken and fashioned into something entirely different. Or, it can just stay where it was discarded, indefinitely. No one is going to mind at all. It's all pie in the sky really.

Setting-off to explore

Despite the lack of a door, I can, if I wish, get out of the shed. I did think about this quite a bit before I first tried it. I simply kneel on the stool, reach over the bench and wiggle at the rusty nail, then keep wiggling, until it springs out! Somehow, it seems to put up the most resistance immediately prior to putting up none-at-all. This is always when you least expect, which generally results in grazed fingers, and the nail bouncing across the bench onto the floor! Then, it all happens quite quickly: the shutters snap upward, with a sharp crack, and the shed fills with blinding light! There's no glass in the window, why would there be?

So, once accustomed to the light, I can carefully clamber over the bench, making sure I don't squash anything on it, until I'm perched on the ledge of the small window. There's a bit of a drop down from here, into the undergrowth, which slopes away from the shed. Picking my moment, I can just launch myself off the ledge and land in the lush vegetation, normally with a bit of a thud, and a shout, as I twist my ankle slightly, but not badly enough to care for more than for the next couple of steps. So, that's it! me, out of the shed!

At this point you may be wondering how I get back into the shed … that's much easier, however. I don't! Or at least I've never had to, as I just wait until my next visit to the island, then land un-salubriously back on my stool, springs groaning. I don't even need to find the nail from on the floor, as the shutters are down and the nail back firmly in place retaining them. I just switch the fan back on and that's it, back to business.

Uncharted territory

I do have a trapdoor in the floor too! It's half under my bench and slightly offset to one side. It has a big, brass padlock on a hasp and, as far as I know, no key … although, there is a key, with a tag, hanging on a nail by the window. I suppose, there's a chance that that may fit, but I've never tried it. I've always been of the opinion that if someone puts a padlock on something its normally to keep honest people out, people like me! Dishonest people, however, only see a padlock as a temporary inconvenience and an in-dication that removing it might be a good idea. The main thing to me about the trapdoor is that it is, indeed, slightly offset to one side. This is great, and well thought out too, as it means that it's not in my way at all when I'm sat working at my bench.

There's a telephone on my bench, it's not a smartphone or anything like that, it's a 'proper' telephone, with a dial, although I don't think it has a bell. I don't *really* know why it's there, I suspect it's there just to make me feel more important, or something like that. I don't think it has a bell as it's never rung. One thing I do know, though, if it ever *does* ring, it's going straight out of the window, shutters or no shutters!

BIRDS ON INDRIEG

The One-eyed Trycrought
v. the Squick

We have a number of seabirds that frequent the island on their way to cooler climates. We do have a few native birds, however, such as the "One-eyed Trycrought". We don't have very many of these birds on Indrieg and I suppose I'm glad in a way. The strangest thing about the One-eyed Trycrought, you'll notice straight away if you see one, is that, they actually have two eyes, just the one leg ... but that's another story. It's generally believed that their name evolved, but they probably didn't ... a cruel twist of irony and fate.

Then, there's the "Squick", which is not a-s-quick as you might think. If one were to have a race with the One-eyed Trycrought it would possibly be neck-and-neck, but that's running on the flat. Flying there'd be absolutely no contest - the Trycrought would have completed a couple of laps of the island before the Squick had stopped laughing for long enough to even take off! They do have this particularly mean sense of humour, especially where Trycroughts are concerned. The Trycroughts by contrast are having none-of-it and look down their noses at the silly Squick, with the greatest of disdain.

◆ ◆ ◆

THE 'UNSCHEDULED DEPARTURE'

How to remain here?

One of the main problems I have with Indrieg, if not *the* problem with Indreig, is staying here, at least for very long.

Let me explain what I mean: I've been coming to Indrieg for a good many years now. I first started coming when I was a child. I can't remember exactly how old I was when I first came. The shed would have model planes hanging on strings from the ceiling, copious amounts of wood dust and shavings with several partially finished models on the bench. There would be a strong smell of cellulose dope and balsa cement, mingled with crayons, because everything smells of crayons when you're a child ... that, and chewed pencils. Back in those days I could easily climb onto my stool, and hop over the models, onto the windowsill, with quite some dexterity ... just couldn't get the rusty nail out which retained the shutters! So, the shutters would remain firmly in place, but I was fine with that as my *models* were on the bench! Why would I need the shutters open? Plenty enough light crept around the side to adequately illuminate my workspace.

What happens on Indrieg, stays on Indrieg ...

I remember once wanting a Mamod steam engine, but my parents said they were too dangerous and that I wasn't old enough to play with fire and steam! So, yes, you can guess it, things were very different on Indrieg - I had a new and exciting project on my bench, directly involving fire and steam! Looking back, I *do* admit they may have had a point, as I *can* remember things getting slightly out-of-hand, resulting in a small fireball and the loss of my eyebrows! But, that didn't matter at all, because what happens on Indrieg *stays* on Indrieg ... it's what happens 'off'

Indrieg that you *really* have to worry about.

AN INCH OR A MILE?

On more occasions than I would care to mention, I'd be carefully gluing the final wing-former in place, on one of my models, when I'd hear my surname, shouted in a very loud, deep and angry sounding voice. Simultaneously, a blackboard eraser would rattle itself around my ears!

"So Ainsworth, would your care to tell the class the exact diameter of the cylinder? No, I thought not! I didn't think Ainsworth could tell the class..."

I'd find myself looking straight into the bright red, wrinkled face of a schoolmaster, with more hair sticking out of his ears and nostrils than he had on the rest of his head, bar the mono-brow. Globules of spit would flick from his mouth and land on me, whilst he continued his fiery discourse. ... I'd just be wondering how he managed to construct sentences with so many words starting with 'p's or 't's ... Then he'd start theatrically stomping about the classroom, making wild gesticulations, with a wooden ruler, in my direction! I'd given him exactly what he was looking for! Now he was in his element, tatty black gown flowing out behind him, as he indulged in his masterful performance. 'Was he *born* this grotesque, or did he have to *practice* to become this grotesque, maybe pushing golf balls up his nostrils whilst, simultaneously, sucking lemons? Is there somewhere you can go to learn to despise children this much... or was this it, was I there and was I part of the project? If I was, it was going terribly well!'

Silence now filled the room, the silence actually feeling louder than the discourse! My teacher, who had stopped his stomping and wild gesticulations, with mono-brow partially raised, now stared straight at me, still anticipating an answer. There was an uncomfortable pause ...

"Is it a mile Sir?" I hesitantly asked.

"Is it a mile!? Is it a mile!? Ainsworth thinks it's a

mile! How could it possibly be a mile!" he spat, "the circumference is only three inches... but Ainsworth thinks the diameter's a mile! "

So, as I say, the problem with Indrieg is *staying* there, or *at least* for very long.

The absent goalie

Throughout my childhood I remember many, frequent, unscheduled departures from Indrieg. I can still hear the 'ping-g-g' noise that is made by a plastic football when kicked at full force and at point-blank range into the cold face of an inattentive goal keeper on a cold frosty morning and following this, the wrath of my unsympathetic team mates, as the ball ricochets firmly into the back of the net!

'Why can't it at least have the decency to ricochet somewhere useful, maybe onto a very sharp pointy object!'

How fast is an inch?

As I grew older, the unscheduled departures remained as frequent, - just the circumstances changed. Whilst contemplating serious issues like 'how much longer would the legs on my stool have to be to reach the floor ..... and if they were that much longer would the floor move further away?' I'd find the shed lighting up with a bright blue flashing light ... Yes, you've guessed it, an imminent unscheduled departure! Winding down my car window I'd find myself saying 'Yes officer!'

"Exactly how fast in a '30' do you imagine you were going sir?'

At this point I can't help suspecting that the schoolmaster has relatives in the force. It wasn't so much his appearance, more the level of questioning. I wasn't falling for this though, clearly the answer was in the question, it's not rocket science or even ' in the sky', I'd been here before.

"Was it an inch officer?" I hesitantly asked.

"Would you kindly step out of your car sir and accompany me to the police vehicle?" came the prompt reply.

Called back to 'reality!'

Since becoming a parent, I've experienced frequent, and to a point, understandable, unscheduled departures from Indrieg, normally starting with a single word, making it across the void, which separates Indrieg from everything that those around me affectionately refer to as reality.

"Dad?"

At this point, it isn't helpful, but with a little concentration, I can resist and remain firmly on my stool, getting on with the business in hand.

"Dad?", now a bit louder, then "DAD!"

'That's it, I'm out of here, like it or not!'

"No, you can't have a steam engine for your birthday, what sort of irresponsible parent would I be, letting my children play with fire and steam!"

THE CONTRACTUAL, UNSCHEDULED, NONE-DEPARTURE

Sometimes, I've learned to resist a departure altogether, just by making an appropriate, occasional, but timely grunt. This, however, has a dark side and that is the 'contractual, unscheduled, none-departure'.

Let me explain: whilst I've been actively and creatively trying to combat the problem with Indrieg, by developing ways to remain here, irrespective of external influences, by muttering the odd 'yes', or something along those lines, my family have been conspiring against me and turning my attempts at remaining, to their advantage. For example, I'm on Indrieg, working hard and I sense words crossing the void and entering my shed. My defence system leaps into 'auto protect' mode. The work I'm doing is very complex and intricate. An interruption at this point could cause the whole thing to go unstable and absolutely anything could happen and I, for one, don't wish to be responsible for the scale of catastrophe that would doubtless follow. I hear myself say

"Hmm yes ..."

It's not so much that 'I' that say it, but more my highly trained defence system, being aware of the delicacy of my situation, leaping to my aid. At that, the issue quickly resolves and peace follows, enabling me to give my fullest concentration to the matter at hand. Deep down I think this to be a triumph, or at least I do, until a couple of days later when my daughter proudly asks me for the £30 that I owe her for her new dress.

"What!' I exclaim, "I never agreed to pay for it..."

"Yes you did, actually," says my wife, leaping to her defence.

So, there you have it! The 'contract' that I've unwittingly entered into, in order to avert an unscheduled departure! Unscheduled departures or 'unscheduled none-departures' always come at a price - the only one, however, that is blissfully unaware of the price, is me, until, that is, I find myself paying it!

ANIMALS ON INDRIEG

T here are many animals indigenous to the island. Most are small, fluffy, squeaky ones, not like mice or rats or anything like that, more like if you took a chipmunk and crossed it with a lemur, whilst adding copious amounts of teddy bear. I don't think we have any larger breeds of animal on the island, or at least, if we do, I've never seen one, but that doesn't mean too much with me. It's quite probable that I'll just finish writing this then see one!

The antics of the fluff-ball-bunny

There's the fluff-ball-bunny, which I'd be tempted to tell you was entirely bald and perched in the trees. Nothing could be further from the truth, however.

They look like little, round rabbits, with big eyes, round ears and have liberal amounts of lush, fluffy fur, although they *do* perch in the trees. They hop from branch to branch, often playing little tig games with one another. These games can go on for hours, especially as they seldom remember who's 'on'. Unlike, say a monkey, that can use its long tail for balance' the fluff-ball-bunny only has a stubby little tail, and frequently loses its balance altogether, falling out of the tree completely, making a 'weeeee' noise as it tumbles down then a dull thud and a small squeak. I don't think it can hurt them too much however, or if so, they have very short memories, as they are soon back in the trees hoping from branch to branch playing tig again.

I'd suggest they played their games over the softer long grass, or had a safety net or something like that, but you just can't reason with a fluff-ball-bunny! No you can't tell them anything, and I don't think it's the language barrier either. When you speak to one, for a moment they stop their game and stare at you. They may raise an eyebrow, and for a fleeting moment, you imagine you have their attention. Then, once you've begun to make your point, they'll raise the other eyebrow, let out a loud screech, do a couple of back flips and continue their game, falling even more frequently, as if to send you the message to just 'mind your own business', - which ironically is the exact reason I'm on Indrieg in the first place.

THINGS YOU WON'T FIND ON INDRIEG

I 've talked a little about some of the things you *can* find on Indreieg, but there are also lots of things you certainly *won't* find too - things like 'emotive intention', finding 'intention' is hard enough. Things like 'despair' or 'failure' will not be found here either.

Success guaranteed!

If things don't appear to work out here, then they are either just discarded, or they become the building blocks for even more bazar and convoluted projects, that could only possibly be conceived from the debris of that, which others may have unwittingly perceived, as 'failure'. The more debris, the more building blocks, the greater the diversity, the greater the scope, from which immeasurable possibilities may arise. It's just recycling really, but without those frustrating blue and green bins, yellow flashing lights and noisy smelly lories.

The perfect escape

It goes without saying that legalism, health and safety, and all that sort of stuff, can't be found here either. I'm sure, should there ever be such as a wisp of a notion, of a 'risk assessment', the entire island would instantly vaporise into a very toxic and sticky mess! Consequentially, such a notion, from a health and safety perspective, would be a *very* bad, and indeed, a counterproductive idea. However, none of this really matters as nothing ever goes wrong - just right - but often in a most unexpected and alarming way!

So, the island's sort of 'self-regulating', providing the perfect environment for fluff-ball-bunnies to play tig, copious amounts of clean air for Trycrought's to soar whilst automatically expelling all those things that in our normal daily life we try so hard to escape. Which, I think, is exactly why I escape to Indreieg - my Island!

'THE END'

or rather the "beginning" ...
or quite possibly both!

They say all good things come to an end, but this one just came to the *'beginning'* ... How can that be?

Over the course of the pages above I've been able to introduce you to some of the many delights of Indrieg. I've also shared a few of its hidden, and indeed, not-so-hidden perils. In all I have shared, however, you can be sure of one thing - and that is I haven't even *begun* to scratch the surface, in fact, I've not even 'scratched the scratch' on the surface ... so many tales to tell, and tales best not told, that still may indeed, *be* told.

As a visitor to my island you've been treated to a glimpse, a bit like that day trip to Venice when you glanced at the Venetian Masks on the Rialto Bridge, as you were swept along by the crowds, and you hurriedly visited St. Mark's Square, snatching a quick coffee outside the Quadri, whilst the music washed over you, before rushing through the back streets, just in time to catch the 18:05 train. You never had the chance to 'just have a look down there' or 'around that corner'. You didn't even get to go on a gondola, what with the length of the queue and *that price*!' But, as you hurried toward the station, you had the overwhelming sense that 'this isn't it'. 'One way or another you'll be back, but next time to immerse yourself.'

Next time, you'll book in somewhere nice, but not silly expensive. You'll wander, aimlessly, down the back streets, stopping to admire the work of a street artist, or lean on a bridge and just watch the water flow by. Next time it will be different!

Next time you'll see the sunset across the lagoon and that's just the thing! The sunset on Indrieg is something to behold, the feeling of the coral sand, washing between your toes, as you paddle in the shallows, whilst discovering why you must, *absolutely never* do that, even if it *does* feel amazing. 'So much to explore ... and together we *can* explore it, so many stones unturned, mixed liberally with stones which, with closer inspection, will assure you they are best left exactly the way-up they already are. Okay, if you like, we'll turn *one* of them, but you can be quite sure you'll not be up for turning another!

Just like *my* visits to Indrieg, with its inherent, unscheduled departures, your visit to Indrieg may be over, but I feel sure, just like *me* you'll be back ... but *next* time you may be able to spend a little longer.

The Beginning!

AFTERWORD

T his volume, "Escape to Indrieg", is just a short story. I see it more like one of those flyers found in the lobby of a hotel, or cast on a coffee-table of a B&B - 'Places to visit in the area' - giving you a pleasant hour or two 'out', whilst relieving you of a few 'bob' of your hard-earned cash. It's given you a bit of an escape from the hustle and bustle of life, before getting back to more pressing matters.

However, this book, despite its small and unassuming nature, has made a massive accomplishment!

It's done something that nothing else has ever done ... it's done something that I never knew could be done ... and now it's done, it can never be undone!

It's crossed the void between Indrieg and reality!

... a bit like a drip from a leaky pipe, falling through

the time-space-continuum only to be regurgitated unceremoniously somewhere in Slough. It's 'popped-up' just where 'popping' would seem most unlikely, just like that drip from the leaky pipe. When your back is turned, it can so easily become a squirt, result-ing in a flood!

During my time spent in Indrieg, I may have penned a few things and those few things, just like old receipts, cast into a drawer, have become quite a pile, the odd title, like "Off-piste on Indrieg" or "The Indrieg Effect" mixed in with even odder titles ... all these in a drawer, in a shed, in Indrieg!

'But I'm sure of one thing ... they'll not be staying there!

ABOUT THE AUTHOR

Daryl Ainsworth

Born in Uttoxeter, in 1960, Daryl quickly learnt that he wasn't an ideal fit for the education system of the day.

As a sufferer of dyslexia, not only did the name of his town seem a cruel twist of irony, but his schooling seemed a cruel twist of everything else!

He quickly developed an escape mechanism, a way to live life to the full, irrespective of the surrounding reality.

Indrieg was born, as yet unnamed, but unbounded! It's from here, he is now able to bring you this volume, and indeed, many more, as his other world unravels.

www.ingramcontent.com/pod-product-compliance
Lightning Source LLC
Chambersburg PA
CBHW070327160726
47999CB00003B/1186